String Quartet

Virginia Woolf

The String Quartet
First published 1921
An Unwritten Novel
First published 1920
The Mark on the Wall
First published 1917
A Haunted House
First published 1921
Blue & Green
First published 1921
Monday or Tuesday
First published 1921
A Society
First published 1921
Kew Gardens
First published 1919
Solid Objects
First published 1920

Cover Art: "String Quartet", by William Meyerowitz

ISBN-10: 1943341028
ISBN-13: 978-1943341023

Contents

"Shamelessly Impressionistic"

"A good deal of the secret of the charm of Mrs Woolf's shorter pieces consists in the immense disparity between the object and the train of feeling which it has set in motion.

Mrs Woolf gives you the minutest datum, and leads you on to explore, quite consciously, the sequence of images and feelings which float away from it.

The result is something which makes Walter Pater appear an unsophisticated rationalist, and the writing is often remarkable.

The book is one of the most curious and interesting examples of a process of dissociation which in that direction, it would seem, cannot be exceeded."

T. S. Eliot

The String Quartet

WELL, here we are, and if you cast your eye over the room you will see that Tubes and trams and omnibuses, private carriages not a few, even, I venture to believe, landaus with bays in them, have been busy at it, weaving threads from one end of London to the other. Yet I begin to have my doubts—

If indeed it's true, as they're saying, that Regent Street is up, and the Treaty signed, and the weather not cold for the time of year, and even at that rent not a flat to be had, and the worst of influenza its after effects; if I bethink me of having forgotten to write about the leak in the larder, and left my glove in the train; if the ties of blood require me, leaning forward, to accept cordially the hand which is perhaps offered hesitatingly—

"Seven years since we met!"

"The last time in Venice."

"And where are you living now?"

"Well, the late afternoon suits me the best, though, if it weren't asking too much——"

"But I knew you at once!"

"Still, the war made a break——"

If the mind's shot through by such little arrows, and—for human society compels it—no sooner is one launched than another presses forward; if this engenders heat and in addition they've turned on the electric light; if saying one thing does, in so many cases, leave behind it a need to improve and revise, stirring besides regrets, pleasures, vanities, and desires—if it's all the facts I mean, and the hats, the fur boas, the gentlemen's swallow-tail coats, and pearl tie-pins that come to the surface—what chance is there?

Of what? It becomes every minute more difficult to say why, in spite of everything, I sit here believing I can't now say what, or even remember the last time it happened.

"Did you see the procession?"

"The King looked cold."

"No, no, no. But what was it?"

"She's bought a house at Malmesbury."

"How lucky to find one!"

On the contrary, it seems to me pretty sure that she, whoever she may be, is damned, since it's all a matter of flats and hats and sea gulls, or so it seems to be for a hundred people sitting here well dressed, walled in, furred, replete.

Not that I can boast, since I too sit passive on a gilt chair, only turning the earth above a buried memory, as we all do, for there are signs, if I'm not mistaken, that we're all recalling something, furtively seeking something.

Why fidget? Why so anxious about the sit of cloaks; and gloves—whether to button or unbutton? Then watch that elderly face against the dark canvas, a moment ago urbane and flushed; now taciturn and sad, as if in shadow.

Was it the sound of the second violin tuning in the ante-room? Here they come; four black figures, carrying instruments, and seat themselves facing the white squares under the downpour of light; rest the tips of their bows on the music stand; with a simultaneous movement lift them; lightly poise them, and, looking across at the player opposite, the first violin counts one, two, three——

Flourish, spring, burgeon, burst! The pear tree on the top of the mountain. Fountains jet; drops descend. But the waters of the Rhone flow swift and deep, race under the arches, and sweep the trailing water leaves, washing shadows over the silver fish, the spotted fish rushed down by the swift waters, now swept into an eddy where—it's difficult this—conglomeration of fish all in a pool; leaping, splashing, scraping sharp fins; and such a boil of current that the yellow pebbles are churned round and round, round and round—free now, rushing downwards, or even somehow ascending in exquisite spirals into the air; curled like thin shavings from under a plane; up and up....

How lovely goodness is in those who, stepping lightly, go smiling through the world! Also in jolly old fishwives, squatted under arches, oh scene old women, how deeply they laugh and shake and rollick, when they walk, from side to side, hum, hah!

"That's an early Mozart, of course——"

"But the tune, like all his tunes, makes one despair —I mean hope. What do I mean? That's the worst of music! I want to dance, laugh, eat pink cakes, yellow cakes, drink thin, sharp wine.

Or an indecent story, now—I could relish that. The older one grows the more one likes indecency. Hall, hah! I'm laughing. What at? You said nothing, nor did the old gentleman opposite.... But suppose—suppose— Hush!"

The melancholy river bears us on. When the moon comes through the trailing willow boughs, I see your face, I hear your voice and the bird singing as we pass the osier bed.

What are you whispering? Sorrow, sorrow. Joy, joy. Woven together, like reeds in moonlight. Woven together, inextricably commingled, bound in pain and strewn in sorrow—crash!

The boat sinks. Rising, the figures ascend, but now leaf thin, tapering to a dusky wraith, which, fiery tipped, draws its twofold passion from my heart. For me it sings, unseals my sorrow, thaws compassion, floods with love the sunless world, nor, ceasing, abates its tenderness but deftly, subtly, weaves in and out until in this pattern, this consummation, the cleft ones unify; soar, sob, sink to rest, sorrow and joy.

Why then grieve? Ask what? Remain unsatisfied? I say all's been settled; yes; laid to rest under a coverlet of rose leaves, falling. Falling. Ah, but they cease. One rose leaf, falling from an enormous height, like a little parachute dropped from an invisible balloon, turns, flutters waveringly. It won't reach us.

"No, no. I noticed nothing. That's the worst of music —these silly dreams. The second violin was late, you say?"

"There's old Mrs. Munro, feeling her way out— blinder each year, poor woman—on this slippery floor."

Eyeless old age, grey-headed Sphinx.... There she stands on the pavement, beckoning, so sternly, the red omnibus.

"How lovely! How well they play! How—how—how!"

The tongue is but a clapper. Simplicity itself. The feathers in the hat next me are bright and pleasing as a child's rattle. The leaf on the plane-tree flashes green through the chink in the curtain. Very strange, very exciting.

"How—how—how!" Hush!

These are the lovers on the grass.

"If, madam, you will take my hand——"

"Sir, I would trust you with my heart. Moreover, we have left our bodies in the banqueting hall. Those on the turf are the shadows of our souls."

"Then these are the embraces of our souls." The lemons nod assent. The swan pushes from the bank and floats dreaming into mid stream.

"But to return. He followed me down the corridor, and, as we turned the corner, trod on the lace of my petticoat. What could I do but cry 'Ah!' and stop to finger it? At which he drew his sword, made passes as if he were stabbing something to death, and cried, 'Mad! Mad! Mad!' Whereupon I screamed, and the Prince, who was writing in the large vellum book in the oriel window, came out in his velvet skull-cap and furred slippers, snatched a rapier from the wall—the King of Spain's gift, you know—on which I escaped, flinging on this cloak to hide the ravages to my skirt—to hide... But listen! the horns!"

The gentleman replies so fast to the lady, and she runs up the scale with such witty exchange of compliment now culminating in a sob of passion, that the words are indistinguishable though the meaning is plain enough—love, laughter, flight, pursuit, celestial bliss—all floated out on the gayest ripple of tender endearment—until the sound of the silver horns, at first far distant, gradually sounds more and more distinctly, as if seneschals were saluting the dawn or proclaiming ominously the escape of the lovers....

The green garden, moonlit pool, lemons, lovers, and fish are all dissolved in the opal sky, across which, as the horns are joined by trumpets and supported by clarions there rise white arches firmly planted on marble pillars....

Tramp and trumpeting. Clang and clangor. Firm establishment. Fast foundations. March of myriads. Confusion and chaos trod to earth.

But this city to which we travel has neither stone nor marble; hangs enduring; stands unshakable; nor does a face, nor does a flag greet or welcome.

Leave then to perish your hope; droop in the desert my joy; naked advance. Bare are the pillars; auspicious to none; casting no shade; resplendent; severe.

Back then I fall, eager no more, desiring only to go, find the street, mark the buildings, greet the apple woman, say to the maid who opens the door: A starry night.

"Good night, good night. You go this way?"

"Alas. I go that."

* * * * *

An Unwritten Novel

SUCH an expression of unhappiness was enough by itself to make one's eyes slide above the paper's edge to the poor woman's face—insignificant without that look, almost a symbol of human destiny with it.

Life's what you see in people's eyes; life's what they learn, and, having learnt it, never, though they seek to hide it, cease to be aware of—what? That life's like that, it seems. Five faces opposite—five mature faces—and the knowledge in each face.

Strange, though, how people want to conceal it! Marks of reticence are on all those faces: lips shut, eyes shaded, each one of the five doing something to hide or stultify his knowledge.

One smokes; another reads; a third checks entries in a pocket book; a fourth stares at the map of the line framed opposite; and the fifth—the terrible thing about the fifth is that she does nothing at all. She looks at life. Ah, but my poor, unfortunate woman, do play the game—do, for all our sakes, conceal it!

As if she heard me, she looked up, shifted slightly in her seat and sighed. She seemed to apologize and at the same time to say to me, "If only you knew!" Then she looked at life again.

"But I do know," I answered silently, glancing at the Times for manners' sake. "I know the whole business. 'Peace between Germany and the Allied Powers was yesterday officially ushered in at Paris—Signor Nitti, the Italian Prime Minister—a passenger train at

Doncaster was in collision with a goods train...' We all know—the Times knows—but we pretend we don't."

My eyes had once more crept over the paper's rim She shuddered, twitched her arm queerly to the middle of her back and shook her head.

Again I dipped into my great reservoir of life. "Take what you like," I continued, "births, deaths, marriages, Court Circular, the habits of birds, Leonardo da Vinci, the Sandhills murder, high wages and the cost of living—oh, take what you like," I repeated, "it's all in the Times!"

Again with infinite weariness she moved her head from side to side until, like a top exhausted with spinning, it settled on her neck.

The Times was no protection against such sorrow as hers. But other human beings forbade intercourse.

The best thing to do against life was to fold the paper so that it made a perfect square, crisp, thick, impervious even to life. This done, I glanced up quickly, armed with a shield of my own.

She pierced through my shield; she gazed into my eyes as if searching any sediment of courage at the depths of them and damping it to clay. Her twitch alone denied all hope, discounted all illusion.

So we rattled through Surrey and across the border into Sussex. But with my eyes upon life I did not see that the other travelers had left, one by one, till, save for the man who read, we were alone together.

Here was Three Bridges station. We drew slowly down the platform and stopped. Was he going to leave us? I prayed both ways—I prayed last that he might stay. At that instant he roused himself, crumpled his paper contemptuously, like a thing done with, burst open the door, and left us alone.

The unhappy woman, leaning a little forward, palely and colorlessly addressed me—talked of stations and holidays, of brothers at Eastbourne, and the time of year, which was, I forget now, early or late.

But at last looking from the window and seeing, I knew, only life, she breathed, "Staying away—that's the drawback of it——" Ah, now we approached the catastrophe, "My sister-in-law"—the bitterness of her tone was like lemon on cold steel, and speaking, not to me, but to herself, she muttered, "nonsense, she would say—that's what they all say," and while she spoke she fidgeted as though the skin on her back were as a plucked fowl's in a poulterer's shop-window.

"Oh, that cow!" she broke off nervously, as though the great wooden cow in the meadow had shocked her and saved her from some indiscretion.

Then she shuddered, and then she made the awkward angular movement that I had seen before, as if, after the spasm, some spot between the shoulders burnt or itched.

Then again she looked the most unhappy woman in the world, and I once more reproached her, though not with the same conviction, for if there were a reason, and if I knew the reason, the stigma was removed from life.

"Sisters-in-law," I said—

Her lips pursed as if to spit venom at the word; pursed they remained. All she did was to take her glove and rub hard at a spot on the window-pane. She rubbed as if she would rub something out for ever— some stain, some indelible contamination.

Indeed, the spot remained for all her rubbing, and back she sank with the shudder and the clutch of the arm I had come to expect.

Something impelled me to take my glove and rub my window. There, too, was a little speck on the glass. For all my rubbing it remained. And then the spasm went through me, I crooked my arm and plucked at the middle of my back. My skin, too, felt like the damp chicken's skin in the poulterer's shop-window; one spot between the shoulders itched and irritated, felt clammy, felt raw. Could I reach it? Surreptitiously I tried.

She saw me. A smile of infinite irony, infinite sorrow, flitted and faded from her face. But she had communicated, shared her secret, passed her poison she would speak no more.

Leaning back in my corner, shielding my eyes from her eyes, seeing only the slopes and hollows, greys and purples, of the winter's landscape, I read her message, deciphered her secret, reading it beneath her gaze.

Hilda's the sister-in-law. Hilda? Hilda? Hilda Marsh —Hilda the blooming, the full bosomed, the matronly. Hilda stands at the door as the cab draws up, holding a coin.

"Poor Minnie, more of a grasshopper than ever—old cloak she had last year. Well, well, with too children these days one can't do more. No, Minnie, I've got it; here you are, cabby—none of your ways with me. Come in, Minnie. Oh, I could carry you, let alone your basket!" So they go into the dining-room. "Aunt Minnie, children."

Slowly the knives and forks sink from the upright. Down they get (Bob and Barbara), hold out hands stiffly; back again to their chairs, staring between the resumed mouthfuls. [But this we'll skip; ornaments, curtains, trefoil china plate, yellow oblongs of cheese, white squares of biscuit—skip—oh, but wait!

Half-way through luncheon one of those shivers; Bob stares at her, spoon in mouth. "Get on with your pudding, Bob;" but Hilda disapproves. "Why should she twitch?" Skip, skip, till we reach the landing on the upper floor; stairs brass-bound; linoleum worn;

oh, yes! little bedroom looking out over the roofs of Eastbourne—zigzagging roofs like the spines of caterpillars, this way, that way, striped red and yellow, with blue-black slating].

Now, Minnie, the door's shut; Hilda heavily descends to the basement; you unstrap the straps of your basket, lay on the bed a meager nightgown, stand side by side furred felt slippers. The looking-glass—no, you avoid the looking-glass.

Some methodical disposition of hat-pins. Perhaps the shell box has something in it? You shake it; it's the pearl stud there was last year—that's all. And then the sniff, the sigh, the sitting by the window.

Three o'clock on a December afternoon; the rain drizzling; one light low in the skylight of a drapery emporium; another high in a servant's bedroom—this one goes out. That gives her nothing to look at.

A moment's blankness—then, what are you thinking? (Let me peep across at her opposite; she's asleep or pretending it; so what would she think about sitting at the window at three o'clock in the afternoon? Health, money, bills, her God?)

Yes, sitting on the very edge of the chair looking over the roofs of Eastbourne, Minnie Marsh prays to Gods. That's all very well; and she may rub the pane too, as though to see God better; but what God does she see? Who's the God of Minnie Marsh, the God of the back streets of Eastbourne, the God of three o'clock in the afternoon?

I, too, see roofs, I see sky; but, oh, dear—this seeing of Gods! More like President Kruger than Prince Albert —that's the best I can do for him; and I see him on a chair, in a black frock-coat, not so very high up either; I can manage a cloud or two for him to sit on; and then his hand trailing in the cloud holds a rod, a truncheon is it?—black, thick, thorned—a brutal old bully—Minnie's God! Did he send the itch and the patch and the twitch? Is that why she prays? What she rubs on the window is the stain of sin. Oh, she committed some crime!

I have my choice of crimes. The woods flit and fly—in summer there are bluebells; in the opening there, when Spring comes, primroses. A parting, was it, twenty years ago? Vows broken? Not Minnie's!... She was faithful. How she nursed her mother! All her savings on the tombstone—wreaths under glass—daffodils in jars. But I'm off the track.

A crime.... They would say she kept her sorrow, suppressed her secret—her sex, they'd say—the scientific people. But what flummery to saddle her with sex! No—more like this.

Passing down the streets of Croydon twenty years ago, the violet loops of ribbon in the draper's window spangled in the electric light catch her eye. She lingers —past six. Still by running she can reach home. She pushes through the glass swing door.

It's sale-time. Shallow trays brim with ribbons. She pauses, pulls this, fingers that with the raised roses on it—no need to choose, no need to buy, and each tray with its surprises.

"We don't shut till seven," and then it is seven. She runs, she rushes, home she reaches, but too late. Neighbors—the doctor— baby brother—the kettle—scalded—hospital—dead—or only the shock of it, the blame?

Ah, but the detail matters nothing! It's what she carries with her; the spot, the crime, the thing to expiate, always there between her shoulders. "Yes," she seems to nod to me, "it's the thing I did."

Whether you did, or what you did, I don't mind; it's not the thing I want. The draper's window looped with violet—that'll do; a little cheap perhaps, a little commonplace—since one has a choice of crimes, but then so many (let me peep across again—still sleeping, or pretending sleep! white, worn, the mouth closed—a touch of obstinacy, more than one would think—no hint of sex)—so many crimes aren't your crime; your crime was cheap; only the retribution solemn; for now the church door opens, the hard wooden pew receives her; on the brown tiles she kneels; every day, winter, summer, dusk, dawn (here she's at it) prays.

All her sins fall, fall, for ever fall. The spot receives them. It's raised, it's red, it's burning. Next she twitches. Small boys point. "Bob at lunch today"—But elderly women are the worst.

Indeed now you can't sit praying any longer. Kruger's sunk beneath the clouds—washed over as with a painter's brush of liquid grey, to which he adds a tinge of black—even the tip of the truncheon gone now. That's what always happens! Just as you've seen him, felt him, someone interrupts. It's Hilda now.

How you hate her! She'll even lock the bathroom door overnight, too, though it's only cold water you want, and sometimes when the night's been bad it seems as if washing helped.

And John at breakfast—the children—meals are worst, and sometimes there are friends—ferns don't altogether hide 'em—they guess, too; so out you go along the front, where the waves are grey, and the papers blow, and the glass shelters green and draughty, and the chairs cost tuppence—too much—for there must be preachers along the sands.

Ah, that's a nigger—that's a funny man—that's a man with parakeets—poor little creatures! Is there no one here who thinks of God?—just up there, over the pier, with his rod—but no—there's nothing but grey in the sky or if it's blue the white clouds hide him, and the music—it's military music—and what they are fishing for? Do they catch them?

How the children stare! Well, then home a back way—"Home a back way!" The words have meaning; might have been spoken by the old man with whiskers—no, no, he didn't really speak; but everything has meaning—placards leaning against doorways—names above shop-windows—red fruit in baskets—women's heads in the hairdresser's—all say "Minnie Marsh!"

But here's a jerk. "Eggs are cheaper!" That's what always happens! I was heading her over the waterfall, straight for madness, when, like a flock of dream sheep, she turns the other way and runs between my fingers.

Eggs are cheaper. Tethered to the shores of the world, none of the crimes, sorrows, rhapsodies, or insanities for poor Minnie Marsh; never late for luncheon; never caught in a storm without a mackintosh; never utterly unconscious of the cheapness of eggs. So she reaches home—scrapes her boots.

Have I read you right? But the human face—the human face at the top of the fullest sheet of print holds more, withholds more.

Now, eyes open, she looks out; and in the human eye—how do you define it?—there's a break—a division—so that when you've grasped the stem the butterfly's off—the moth that hangs in the evening over the yellow flower—move, raise your hand, off, high, away.

I won't raise my hand. Hang still, then, quiver, life, soul, spirit, whatever you are of Minnie Marsh—I, too, on my flower—the hawk over the down—alone, or what were the worth of life?

To rise; hang still in the evening, in the midday; hang still over the down. The flicker of a hand—off, up! then poised again. Alone, unseen; seeing all so still down there, all so lovely.

None seeing, none caring. The eyes of others our prisons; their thoughts our cages. Air above, air below. And the moon and immortality....

Oh, but I drop to the turf! Are you down too, you in the corner, what's your name—woman—Minnie Marsh; some such name as that?

There she is, tight to her blossom; opening her hand-bag, from which she takes a hollow shell—an egg —who was saying that eggs were cheaper? You or I?

Oh, it was you who said it on the way home, you remember, when the old gentleman, suddenly opening his umbrella—or sneezing was it?

Anyhow, Kruger went, and you came "home a back way," and scraped your boots. Yes. And now you lay across your knees a pocket-handkerchief into which drop little angular fragments of eggshell—fragments of a map—a puzzle.

I wish I could piece them together! If you would only sit still. She's moved her knees—the map's in bits again. Down the slopes of the Andes the white blocks of marble go bounding and hurtling, crushing to death a whole troop of Spanish muleteers, with their convoy —Drake's booty, gold and silver. But to return——

To what, to where? She opened the door, and, putting her umbrella in the stand—that goes without saying; so, too, the whiff of beef from the basement; dot, dot, dot.

But what I cannot thus eliminate, what I must, head down, eyes shut, with the courage of a battalion and the blindness of a bull, charge and disperse are, indubitably, the figures behind the ferns, commercial travelers.

There I've hidden them all this time in the hope that somehow they'd disappear, or better still emerge, as indeed they must, if the story's to go on gathering richness and rotundity, destiny and tragedy, as stories should, rolling along with it two, if not three, commercial travelers and a whole grove of aspidistra.

"The fronds of the aspidistra only partly concealed the commercial traveler—" Rhododendrons would conceal him utterly, and into the bargain give me my fling of red and white, for which I starve and strive; but rhododendrons in Eastbourne—in December—on the Marshes' table—no, no, I dare not; it's all a matter of crusts and cruets, frills and ferns.

Perhaps there'll be a moment later by the sea. Moreover, I feel, pleasantly pricking through the green fretwork and over the glacis of cut glass, a desire to peer and peep at the man opposite—one's as much as I can manage.

James Moggridge is it, whom the Marshes call Jimmy? [Minnie, you must promise not to twitch till I've got this straight]. James Moggridge travels in— shall we say buttons?—but the time's not come for bringing them in—the big and the little on the long cards, some peacock-eyed, others dull gold; cairngorms some, and others coral sprays—but I say the time's not come.

He travels, and on Thursdays, his Eastbourne day, takes his meals with the Marshes. His red face, his little steady eyes—by no means. altogether commonplace—his enormous appetite (that's safe; he won't look at Minnie till the bread's swamped the gravy dry), napkin tucked diamond-wise—but this is primitive, and, whatever it may do the reader, don't take me in.

Let's dodge to the Moggridge household, set that in motion. Well, the family boots are mended on Sundays by James himself.

He reads Truth. But his passion? Roses—and his wife a retired hospital nurse—interesting—for God's sake let me have one woman with a name I like!

But no; she's of the unborn children of the mind, illicit, none the less loved, like my rhododendrons. How many die in every novel that's written—the best, the dearest, while Moggridge lives. It's life's fault.

Here's Minnie eating her egg at the moment opposite and at the other end of the line—are we past Lewes?—there must be Jimmy—or what's her twitch for?

There must be Moggridge—life's fault. Life imposes her laws; life blocks the way; life's behind the fern; life's the tyrant; oh, but not the bully! No, for I assure you I come willingly; I come wooed by Heaven knows what compulsion across ferns and cruets, table splashed and bottles smeared.

I come irresistibly to lodge myself somewhere on the firm flesh, in the robust spine, wherever I can penetrate or find foothold on the person, in the soul, of Moggridge the man.

The enormous stability of the fabric; the spine tough as whalebone, straight as oak tree; the ribs radiating branches; the flesh taut tarpaulin; the red hollows; the suck and regurgitation of the heart; while from above meat falls in brown cubes and beer gushes to be churned to blood again—and so we reach the eyes.

Behind the aspidistra they see something: black, white, dismal; now the plate again; behind the aspidistra they see elderly woman; "Marsh's sister, Hilda's more my sort;" the tablecloth now.

"Marsh would know what's wrong with Morrises..." talk that over; cheese has come; the plate again; turn it round—the enormous fingers; now the woman opposite.

"Marsh's sister—not a bit like Marsh; wretched, elderly female.... You should feed your hens.... God's truth, what's set her twitching? Not what I said?

Dear, dear, dear! these elderly women. Dear, dear!"

[Yes, Minnie; I know you've twitched, but one moment—James Moggridge].

"Dear, dear, dear!" How beautiful the sound is! like the knock of a mallet on seasoned timber, like the throb of the heart of an ancient whaler when the seas press thick and the green is clouded.

"Dear, dear!" what a passing bell for the souls of the fretful to soothe them and solace them, lap them in linen, saying, "So long. Good luck to you!" and then, "What's your pleasure?" for though Moggridge would pluck his rose for her, that's done, that's over.

Now what's the next thing? "Madam, you'll miss your train," for they don't linger.

That's the man's way; that's the sound that reverberates; that's St. Paul's and the motor-omnibuses. But we're brushing the crumbs off.

Oh, Moggridge, you won't stay? You must be off? Are you driving through Eastbourne this afternoon in one of those little carriages?

Are you man who's walled up in green cardboard boxes, and sometimes has the blinds down, and sometimes sits so solemn staring like a sphinx, and always there's a look of the sepulchral, something of the undertaker, the coffin, and the dusk about horse and driver? Do tell me—but the doors slammed. We shall never meet again. Moggridge, farewell!

Yes, yes, I'm coming. Right up to the top of the house. One moment I'll linger.

How the mud goes round in the mind—what a swirl these monsters leave, the waters rocking, the weeds waving and green here, black there, striking to the sand, till by degrees the atoms reassemble, the deposit sifts itself, and again through the eyes one sees clear and still, and there comes to the lips some prayer for the departed, some obsequy for the souls of those one nods to, the people one never meets again.

James Moggridge is dead now, gone for ever. Well, Minnie—"I can face it no longer." If she said that—(Let me look at her. She is brushing the eggshell into deep declivities).

She said it certainly, leaning against the wall of the bedroom, and plucking at the little balls which edge the claret-colored curtain.

But when the self speaks to the self, who is speaking?—the entombed soul, the spirit driven in, in, in to the central catacomb; the self that took the veil and left the world—a coward perhaps, yet somehow beautiful, as it flits with its lantern restlessly up and down the dark corridors.

"I can bear it no longer," her spirit says. "That man at lunch—Hilda—the children." Oh, heavens, her sob! It's the spirit wailing its destiny, the spirit driven hither, thither, lodging on the diminishing carpets— meagre footholds—shrunken shreds of all the vanishing universe—love, life, faith, husband, children, I know not what splendors and pageantries glimpsed in girlhood. "Not for me—not for me."

But then—the muffins, the bald elderly dog? Bead mats I should fancy and the consolation of under linen.

If Minnie Marsh were run over and taken to hospital, nurses and doctors themselves would exclaim.... There's the vista and the vision—there's the distance—the blue blot at the end of the avenue, while, after all, the tea is rich, the muffin hot, and the dog —"Benny, to your basket, sir, and see what mother's brought you!"

So, taking the glove with the worn thumb, defying once more the encroaching demon of what's called going in holes, you renew the fortifications, threading the grey wool, running it in and out.

Running it in and out, across and over, spinning a web through which God himself—hush, don't think of God!

How firm the stitches are! You must be proud of your darning. Let nothing disturb her. Let the light fall gently, and the clouds show an inner vest of the first green leaf.

Let the sparrow perch on the twig and shake the raindrop hanging to the twig's elbow.... Why look up?

Was it a sound, a thought? Oh, heavens! Back again to the thing you did, the plate glass with the violet loops? But Hilda will come. Ignominies, humiliations, oh! Close the breach.

Having mended her glove, Minnie Marsh lays it in the drawer. She shuts the drawer with decision. I catch sight of her face in the glass. Lips are pursed. Chin held high.

Next she laces her shoes. Then she touches her throat. What's your brooch? Mistletoe or merrythought? And what is happening? Unless I'm much mistaken, the pulse's quickened, the moment's coming, the threads are racing, Niagara's ahead.

Here's the crisis! Heaven be with you! Down she goes. Courage, courage! Face it, be it! For God's sake don't wait on the mat now! There's the door! I'm on your side. Speak! Confront her, confound her soul!

"Oh, I beg your pardon! Yes, this is Eastbourne. I'll reach it down for you. Let me try the handle." [But, Minnie, though we keep up pretences, I've read you right—I'm with you now].

"That's all your luggage?"

"Much obliged, I'm sure."

(But why do you look about you? Hilda don't come to the station, nor John; and Moggridge is driving at the far side of Eastbourne).

"I'll wait by my bag, ma'am, that's safest. He said he'd meet me.... Oh, there he is! That's my son."

So they walk off together.

Well, but I'm confounded.... Surely, Minnie, you know better! A strange young man.... Stop! I'll tell him —Minnie!—Miss Marsh!—I don't know though.

There's something queer in her cloak as it blows. Oh, but it's untrue, it's indecent.... Look how he bends as they reach the gateway.

She finds her ticket. What's the joke? Off they go, down the road, side by side.... Well, my world's done for! What do I stand on? What do I know? That's not Minnie. There never was Moggridge. Who am I? Life's bare as bone.

And yet the last look of them—he stepping from the kerb and she following him round the edge of the big building brims me with wonder—floods me anew.

Mysterious figures! Mother and son. Who are you? Why do you walk down the street? Where tonight will you sleep, and then, tomorrow?

Oh, how it whirls and surges—floats me afresh! I start after them. People drive this way and that. The white light splutters and pours.

Plate-glass windows. Carnations; chrysanthemums. Ivy in dark gardens. Milk carts at the door. Wherever I go, mysterious figures, I see you, turning the corner, mothers and sons; you, you, you.

I hasten, I follow. This, I fancy, must be the sea. Grey is the landscape; dim as ashes; the water murmurs and moves.

If I fall on my knees, if I go through the ritual, the ancient antics, it's you, unknown figures, you I adore; if I open my arms, it's you I embrace, you I draw to me —adorable world!

* * * * *

Virginia Woolf

The Mark on the Wall

PERHAPS it was the middle of January in the present year that I first looked up and saw the mark on the wall.

In order to fix a date it is necessary to remember what one saw. So now I think of the fire; the steady film of yellow light upon the page of my book; the three chrysanthemums in the round glass bowl on the mantelpiece.

Yes, it must have been the winter time, and we had just finished our tea, for I remember that I was smoking a cigarette when I looked up and saw the mark on the wall for the first time.

I looked up through the smoke of my cigarette and my eye lodged for a moment upon the burning coals, and that old fancy of the crimson flag flapping from the castle tower came into my mind, and I thought of the cavalcade of red knights riding up the side of the black rock.

Rather to my relief the sight of the mark interrupted the fancy, for it is an old fancy, an automatic fancy, made as a child perhaps.

The mark was a small round mark, black upon the white wall, about six or seven inches above the mantelpiece.

How readily our thoughts swarm upon a new object, lifting it a little way, as ants carry a blade of straw so feverishly, and then leave it....

Virginia Woolf

If that mark was made by a nail, it can't have been for a picture, it must have been for a miniature, the miniature of a lady with white powdered curls, powder-dusted cheeks, and lips like red carnations.

A fraud of course, for the people who had this house before us would have chosen pictures in that way; an old picture for an old room.

That is the sort of people they were--very interesting people, and I think of them so often, in such queer places, because one will never see them again, never know what happened next.

She wore a flannel collar round her throat, and he drew posters for an oatmeal company, and they wanted to leave this house because they wanted to change their style of furniture, so he said, and he was in process of saying that in his opinion art should have ideas behind it when we were torn asunder, as one is torn from the old lady about to pour out tea and the young man about to hit the tennis ball in the back garden of the suburban villa as one rushes past in the train.

But as for that mark, I'm not sure about it; I don't believe it was made by a nail after all; it's too big, too round, for that.

I might get up, but if I got up and looked at it, ten to one I shouldn't be able to say for certain; because once a thing's done, no one ever knows how it happened. O dear me, the mystery of life! The inaccuracy of thought! The ignorance of humanity!

To show how very little control of our possessions we have— what an accidental affair this living is after all our civilization— let me just count over a few of the things lost in one lifetime, beginning, for that seems always the most mysterious of losses— what cat would gnaw, what rat would nibble three pale blue canisters of bookbinding tools?

Then there were the bird cages, the iron hoops, the steel skates, the Queen Anne coal-scuttle, the bagatelle board, the hand organ— all gone, and jewels too.

Opals and emeralds, they lie about the roots of turnips. What a scraping paring affair it is to be sure!

The wonder is that I've any clothes on my back, that I sit surrounded by solid furniture at this moment.

Why, if one wants to compare life to anything, one must liken it to being blown through the Tube at fifty miles an hour landing at the other end without a single hairpin in one's hair! Shot out at the feet of God entirely naked!

Tumbling head over heels in the asphodel meadows like brown paper parcels pitched down a shoot in the post office! With one's hair flying back like the tail of a race-horse.

Yes, that seems to express the rapidity of life, the perpetual waste and repair; all so casual, all so haphazard. . . .

But after life. The slow pulling down of thick green stalks so that the cup of the flower, as it turns over, deluges one with purple and red light.

Why, after all, should one not be born there as one is born here, helpless, speechless, unable to focus one's eyesight, groping at the roots of the grass, at the toes of the Giants?

As for saying which are trees, and which are men and women, or whether there are such things, that one won't be in a condition to do for fifty years or so.

There will be nothing but spaces of light and dark, intersected by thick stalks, and rather higher up perhaps, rose-shaped blots of an indistinct color dim pinks and blues which will, as time goes on, become more definite, become I don't know what. . . .

And yet that mark on the wall is not a hole at all. It may even be caused by some round black substance, such as a small rose leaf, left over from the summer, and I, not being a very vigilant housekeeper— look at the dust on the mantelpiece, for example, the dust which, so they say, buried Troy three times over, only fragments of pots utterly refusing annihilation, as one can believe.

... I know a housekeeper, a woman with the profile of a policeman, those little round buttons marked even upon the edge of her shadow, a woman with a broom in her hand, a thumb on picture frames, an eye under beds, and she talks always of art.

She is coming nearer and nearer; and now, pointing to certain spots of yellow rust on the fender, she becomes so menacing that to oust her, I shall have to end her by taking action: I shall have to get up and see for myself what that mark—

But no. I refuse to be beaten. I will not move. I will not recognize her. See, she fades already. I am very nearly rid of her and her insinuations, which I can hear quite distinctly. Yet she has about her the pathos of all people who wish to compromise.

And why should I resent the fact that she has a few books in her house, a picture or two? But what I really resent is that she resents me— life being an affair of attack and defense after all. Another time I will have it out with her, —not now. She must go now. . . .

The tree outside the window taps very gently on the pane....

I want to think quietly, calmly, spaciously, never to be interrupted, never to have to rise from my chair, to slip easily from one thing to another, without any sense of hostility, or obstacle. I want to sink deeper and deeper, away from the surface, with its hard separate facts.

To steady myself, let me catch hold of the first idea that passes. . . .

Shakespeare. . . . Well, he will do as well as another.

A man who sat himself solidly in an armchair, and looked into the fire, so—. A shower of ideas fell perpetually from some very high Heaven down through his mind.

He leaned his forehead on his hand, and people, looking in through the open door,— for this scene is supposed to take place on a summer's evening,— But how dull this is, this historical fiction! It doesn't interest me at all.

I wish I could hit upon a pleasant track of thought, a track indirectly reflecting credit upon myself, for those are the pleasantest thoughts, and very frequent even in the minds of modest mouse-colored people, who believe genuinely that they dislike to hear their own praises.

They are not thoughts directly praising oneself; that is the beauty of them ; they are thoughts like this :

"And then I came into the room. They were discussing botany. I said how I'd seen a flower growing on a dust heap on the site of an old house in Kingsway.

The seed, I said, must have been sown in the reign of Charles the First. What flowers grew in the reign of Charles the First? I asked (but I don't remember the answer). Tall flowers with purple tassels to them perhaps.

And so it goes on. All the time I'm dressing up the figure of myself in my own mind, lovingly, stealthily, not openly adoring it, for if I did that, I should catch myself out, and stretch my hand at once for a book in self-protection.

Indeed, it is curious how instinctively one protects

the image of oneself from idolatry or any other handling that could make it ridiculous, or too unlike the original to be believed in any longer.

Or is it not so very curious after all? It is a matter of great importance. Suppose the looking glass smashes, the image disappears, and the romantic figure with the green of forest depths all about it is there no longer, but only that shell of a person which is seen by other people— what an airless, shallow, bald, prominent world it becomes!

A world not to be lived in. As we face each other in omnibuses and underground railways we are looking into the mirror; that accounts for the expression of vagueness, the gleam of glassiness, in our eyes.

And the novelists in future will realize more and more the importance of these reflections, for of course there is not one reflection but an almost infinite number; those are the depths they will explore, those the phantoms they will pursue, leaving the description of reality more and more out of their stories, taking a knowledge of it for granted, as the Greeks did and Shakespeare perhaps— but these generalizations are very worthless.

The military sound of the word is enough. It recalls leading articles, cabinet ministers a whole class of things indeed which as a child one thought the thing itself, the standard thing, the real thing, from which one could not depart save at the risk of nameless damnation.

Generalizations bring back somehow Sunday in London, Sunday afternoon walks, Sunday luncheons, and also ways of speaking of the dead, clothes, and habits like the habit of sitting all together in one room until a certain hour, although nobody liked it.

There was a rule for everything. The rule for tablecloths at that particular period was that they should be made of tapestry with little yellow compartments marked upon them, such as you may see in photographs of the carpets in the corridors of the royal palaces. Tablecloths of a different kind were not real tablecloths.

How shocking, and yet how wonderful it was to discover that these real things, Sunday luncheons, Sunday walks, country houses, and tablecloths were not entirely real, were indeed half phantoms, and the damnation which visited the disbeliever in them was only a sense of illegitimate freedom.

What now takes the place of those things, I wonder, those real standard things? Men perhaps, should you be a woman; the masculine point of view which governs our lives, which sets the standard, which establishes Whitaker's Table of Precedency, which has become, I suppose, since the war half a phantom to many men and women, which soon, one may hope, will be laughed into the dustbin where the phantoms go, the mahogany sideboards and Landseer prints, Gods and Devils, Hell and so forth, leaving us all with an intoxicating sense of illegitimate freedom— if freedom exists. . . .

In certain lights, that mark on the wall seems actually to project from the wall. Nor is it entirely circular. I cannot be sure, but it seems to cast a perceptible shadow, suggesting that if I ran my finger down that strip of the wall it would, at a certain point, mount and descend a small tumulus, a smooth tumulus like those barrows on the South Downs which are, they say, either tombs or camps.

Of the two I should prefer them to be tombs, desiring melancholy like most English people and finding it natural at the end of a walk to think of the bones stretched beneath the turf. . . .

There must be some book about it. Some antiquary must have dug up those bones and given them a name. . . . What sort of man is an antiquary, I wonder?

Retired colonels for the most part, I daresay, leading parties of aged laborers to the top here, examining clods of earth and stone, and getting into correspondence with the neighboring clergy, which, being opened at breakfast time, gives them a feeling of importance, and the comparison of arrow-heads necessitates cross-country journeys to the county towns, an agreeable necessity both to them and to their elderly wives, who wish to make plum jam, or to clean out the study, and have every reason for keeping that great question of the camp or the tomb in perpetual suspension, while the Colonel himself feels agreeably philosophic in accumulating evidence on both sides of the question.

It is true that he does finally incline to believe in the camp; and, being opposed, casts all his arrowheads into one scale, and being still further opposed, indites a pamphlet which he is about to read at the quarterly meeting of the local society when a stroke lays him low, and his last conscious thoughts are not of wife or child, but of the camp and that arrowhead there, which is now in the case at the local museum, together with the foot of a Chinese murderess, a handful of Elizabethan nails, a great many Tudor clay pipes, a piece of Roman pottery, and the wine-glass that Nelson drank out of— proving I really don't know what.

No, no, nothing is proved, nothing is known. And if I Were "to get up at this very moment and ascertain that the mark on the wall is really what shall we say? the head of a gigantic old nail, driven in two hundred years ago, which has now, owing to the patient attrition of many generations of housemaids, revealed its head above the coat of paint, and is taking its first view of modern life in the sight of a white-walled fire-lit room, what should I gain? Knowledge? Matter for further speculation?

I can think sitting still as well as standing up. And what is knowledge? What are our learned men save the descendants of witches and hermits who crouched in caves and in woods brewing herbs, interrogating shrew-mice, and writing down the language of the stars?

And the less we honor them as our superstitions dwindle and our respect for beauty and health of mind increases. . . . Yes, one could imagine a very pleasant world. A quiet spacious world, with the flowers so red and blue in the open fields.

A world without professors or specialists or housekeepers with the profiles of policemen, a world which one could slice with one's thought as a fish slices the water with his fin, grazing the stems of the water-lilies, hanging suspended over nests of white sea eggs. . . .

How peaceful it is down here, rooted into the center of the world and gazing up through the gray waters, with their sudden gleams of light, and their reflections — If it were not for Whitaker's Almanack— if it were not for the Table of Precedency!

I must jump up and see for myself what that mark on the wall really is— a nail, a rose-leaf, a crack in the wood?

Here is Nature once more at her old game of self-preservation. This train of thought, she perceives, is threatening mere waste of energy, even some collision with reality, for who will ever be able to lift a finger against Whitaker's Table of Precedency?

The Archbishop of Canterbury is followed by the Lord High Chancellor; the Lord High Chancellor is followed by the Archbishop of York.

Everybody follows somebody, such is the philosophy of Whitaker; and the great thing is to know who follows whom.

Whitaker knows, and let that, so Nature counsels, comfort you, instead of enraging you; and if you can't be comforted, if you must shatter this hour of peace, think of the mark on the wall.

I understand Nature's game— her prompting to take action as a way of ending any thought that threatens to excite or to pain.

Hence, I suppose, comes our slight contempt for men of action— men, we assume, who don't think. Still, there's no harm in putting a full stop to one's disagreeable thoughts by looking at a mark on the wall.

Indeed, now that I have fixed my eyes upon it, I feel I have grasped a plank in the sea; I feel a satisfying sense of reality which at once turns the two Archbishops and the Lord High Chancellor to the shadows of shades.

Here is something definite, something real. Thus, waking from a midnight dream of horror one hastily turns on the light and lies quiescent, worshiping the chest of drawers, worshiping solidity, worshiping reality, worshiping the impersonal world which is a proof of some existence other than ours.

That is what one wants to be sure of.... Wood is a pleasant thing to think about. It comes from a tree; and trees grow, and we don't know how they grow. For years and years they grow, without paying any attention to us, in meadows, in forests and by the side of rivers— all things one likes to think about.

The cows swish their tails beneath them on hot afternoons; they paint rivers so green that when a moorhen dives one expects to see its feathers all green when it comes up again.

I like to think of the fish balanced against the stream like flags blown out; and of water-beetles slowly raising domes of mud upon the bed of the river.

I like to think of the tree itself; first the close dry sensation of being wood; then there is the grinding of the storm; then the slow, delicious ooze of sap.

I like to think of it, too, on winter's nights standing in the empty field with all leaves close-furled, nothing tender exposed to the iron bullets of the moon, a naked mast upon an earth that goes tumbling, tumbling, all night long.

The song of birds must sound very loud and strange in June; and how cold the feet of insects must feel upon it, as they make laborious progresses up the creases of the bark, or sun themselves upon the thin green awning of the leaves, and look straight in front of them with huge diamond-cut red eyes. . . .

One by one the fibers snap beneath the immense cold pressure of the earth; then the last storm comes and, falling, the highest branches drive deep into the ground again.

Even so, life isn't done with; there are a million patient, watchful, lives still for a tree, all over the world, in bedrooms, in ships, on the pavement, lining rooms where men and women sit after tea, smoking their cigarettes.

It is full of peaceful thoughts, happy thoughts, this tree. I should like to take each one separately but something is getting in the way. . . .

Where was I? What has it all been about? A tree? A river? The Downs, Whitaker's Almanack, the fields of asphodel?

I can't remember a thing.

Everything's moving, falling, slipping, vanishing.... There is a vast upheaval of matter.

Someone is standing over me and saying—

"I'm going out to buy a newspaper."

"Yes?"

"Though it's no good, buying newspapers.... Nothing ever happens. Curse this war! Goddamn this war!.... All the same, I don't see why we should have a snail on our wall."

Ah, the mark on the wall ! It was a snail.

* * * *

A Haunted House

WHATEVER hour you woke there was a door shunting. From room to room they went, hand in hand, lifting here, opening there, making sure—a ghostly couple.

"Here we left it," she said. And he added, "Oh, but here too!" "It's upstairs," she murmured. "And in the garden," he whispered "Quietly," they said, "or we shall wake them."

But it wasn't that you woke us. Oh, no. "They're looking for it; they're drawing the curtain, one might say, and so read on a page or two. "Now they've found it," one would be certain, stopping the pencil on the margin.

And then, tired of reading, one might rise and see for oneself, the house all empty, the doors standing open, only the wood pigeons bubbling with content and the hum of the threshing machine sounding from the farm.

"What did I come in here for? What did I want to find?" My hands were empty. "Perhaps it's upstairs then?"

The apples were in the loft. And so down again, the garden still as ever, only the book had slipped into the grass.

But they had found it in the drawing room. Not that one could ever see them. The window panes reflected apples, reflected roses; all the leaves were green in the glass. If they moved in the drawing room, the apple only turned its yellow side.

Yet, the moment after, if the door was opened, spread about the floor, hung upon the walls, pendant from the ceiling—what?

My hands were empty. The shadow of a thrush crossed the carpet; from the deepest wells of silence the wood pigeon drew its bubble of sound.

"Safe, safe, safe," the pulse of the house beat softly. "The treasure buried; the room..." the pulse stopped short. Oh, was that the buried treasure?

A moment later the light had faded. Out in the garden then? But the trees spun darkness for a wandering beam of sun. So fine, so rare, coolly sunk beneath the surface the beam I sought always burnt behind the glass.

Death was the glass; death was between us; coming to the woman first, hundreds of years ago, leaving the house, sealing all the windows; the rooms were darkened.

He left it, left her, went North, went East, saw the stars turned in the Southern sky; sought the house, found it dropped beneath the Downs.

"Safe, safe, safe," the pulse of the house beat gladly. "The Treasure yours."

The wind roars up the avenue. Trees stoop and bend this way and that. Moonbeams splash and spill wildly in the rain. But the beam of the lamp falls straight from the window.

The candle burns stiff and still. Wandering through the house, opening the windows, whispering not to wake us, the ghostly couple seek their joy.

"Here we slept," she says. And he adds, "Kisses without number." "Waking in the morning—" "Silver between the trees—" "Upstairs—" "In the garden—" "When summer came—" "In winter snow time—" The doors go shutting far in the distance, gently knocking like the pulse of a heart.

Nearer they come; cease at the doorway. The wind falls, the rain slides silver down the glass. Our eyes darken; we hear no steps beside us; we see no lady spread her ghostly cloak. His hands shield the lantern. "Look," he breathes. "Sound asleep. Love upon their lips."

Stooping, holding their silver lamp above us, long they look and deeply. Long they pause. The wind drives straightly; the flame stoops slightly. Wild beams of moonlight cross both floor and wall, and, meeting, stain the faces bent; the faces pondering; the faces that search the sleepers and seek their hidden joy.

"Safe, safe, safe," the heart of the house beats proudly.

"Long years—" he sighs. "Again you found me."

"Here," she murmurs, "sleeping; in the garden reading; laughing, rolling apples in the loft. Here we left our treasure—" Stooping, their light lifts the lids upon my eyes.

"Safe! safe! safe!" the pulse of the house beats wildly.

Waking, I cry "Oh, is this your buried treasure? The light in the heart."

* * * * *

Blue & Green

Green

The ported fingers of glass hang downwards. The light slides down the glass, and drops a pool of green. All day long the ten fingers of the lustre drop green upon the marble.

The feathers of parakeets—their harsh cries—sharp blades of palm trees—green, too; green needles glittering in the sun.

But the hard glass drips on to the marble; the pools hover above the dessert sand; the camels lurch through them; the pools settle on the marble; rushes edge them; weeds clog them; here and there a white blossom; the frog flops over; at night the stars are set there unbroken.

Evening comes, and the shadow sweeps the green over the mantelpiece; the ruffled surface of ocean.

No ships come; the aimless waves sway beneath the empty sky.

It's night; the needles drip blots of blue. The green's out.

Blue

The snub-nosed monster rises to the surface and spouts through his blunt nostrils two columns of water, which, fiery-white in the center, spray off into a fringe of blue beads.

Strokes of blue line the black tarpaulin of his hide. Slushing the water through mouth and nostrils he sings, heavy with water, and the blue closes over him dowsing the polished pebbles of his eyes.

Thrown upon the beach he lies, blunt, obtuse, shedding dry blue scales. Their metallic blue stains the rusty iron on the beach. Blue are the ribs of the wrecked rowing boat.

A wave rolls beneath the blue bells. But the cathedral's different, cold, incense laden, faint blue with the veils of Madonnas.

* * * * *

Monday or Tuesday

LAZY and indifferent, shaking space easily from his wings, knowing his way, the heron passes over the church beneath the sky. White and distant, absorbed in itself, endlessly the sky covers and uncovers, moves and remains.

A lake? Blot the shores of it out! A mountain? Oh, perfect—the sun gold on its slopes. Down that falls. Ferns then, or white feathers, for ever and ever——

Desiring truth, awaiting it, laboriously distilling a few words, for ever desiring—(a cry starts to the left, another to the right. Wheels strike divergently. Omnibuses conglomerate in conflict)—for ever desiring —(the clock asseverates with twelve distinct strokes that it is midday; light sheds gold scales; children swarm)—for ever desiring truth.

Red is the dome; coins hang on the trees; smoke trails from the chimneys; bark, shout, cry "Iron for sale"—and truth?

Radiating to a point men's feet and women's feet, black or gold-encrusted—(This foggy weather—Sugar? No, thank you—The commonwealth of the future)—the firelight darting and making the room red, save for the black figures and their bright eyes, while outside a van discharges,

Miss Thingummy drinks tea at her desk, and plate-glass preserves fur coats——

Flaunted, leaf-light, drifting at corners, blown across the wheels, silver-splashed, home or not home, gathered, scattered, squandered in separate scales, swept up, down, torn, sunk, assembled—and truth?

Now to recollect by the fireside on the white square of marble. From ivory depths words rising shed their blackness, blossom and penetrate.

Fallen the book; in the flame, in the smoke, in the momentary sparks—or now voyaging, the marble square pendant, minarets beneath and the Indian seas, while space rushes blue and stars glint—truth? content with closeness?

Lazy and indifferent the heron returns; the sky veils her stars; then bares them.

* * * * *

A Society

THIS is how it all came about. Six or seven of us were sitting one day after tea. Some were gazing across the street into the windows of a milliner's shop where the light still shone brightly upon scarlet feathers and golden slippers.

Others were idly occupied in building little towers of sugar upon the edge of the tea tray. After a time, so far as I can remember, we drew round the fire and began as usual to praise men—how strong, how noble, how brilliant, how courageous, how beautiful they were— how we envied those who by hook or by crook managed to get attached to one for life—when Poll, who had said nothing, burst into tears.

Poll, I must tell you, has always been queer. For one thing her father was a strange man. He left her a fortune in his will, but on condition that she read all the books in the London Library.

We comforted her as best we could; but we knew in our hearts how vain it was. For though we like her, Poll is no beauty; leaves her shoe laces untied; and must have been thinking, while we praised men, that not one of them would ever wish to marry her.

At last she dried her tears. For some time we could make nothing of what she said. Strange enough it was in all conscience.

She told us that, as we knew, she spent most of her time in the London Library, reading. She had begun, she said, with English literature on the top floor; and was steadily working her way down to the Times on the bottom. And now half, or perhaps only a quarter, way through a terrible thing had happened. She could read no more.

Books were not what we thought them. "Books," she cried, rising to her feet and speaking with an intensity of desolation which I shall never forget, "are for the most part unutterably bad!"

Of course we cried out that Shakespeare wrote books, and Milton and Shelley.

"Oh, yes," she interrupted us. "You've been well taught, I can see. But you are not members of the London Library." Here her sobs broke forth anew.

At length, recovering a little, she opened one of the pile of books which she always carried about with her —"From a Window" or "In a Garden," or some such name as that it was called, and it was written by a man called Benton or Henson, or something of that kind.

She read the first few pages. We listened in silence. "But that's not a book," someone said. So she chose another. This time it was a history, but I have forgotten the writer's name. Our trepidation increased as she went on. Not a word of it seemed to be true, and the style in which it was written was execrable.

"Poetry! Poetry!" we cried, impatiently.

"Read us poetry!" I cannot describe the desolation which fell upon us as she opened a little volume and mouthed out the verbose, sentimental foolery which it contained.

"It must have been written by a woman," one of us urged. But no. She told us that it was written by a young man, one of the most famous poets of the day.

I leave you to imagine what the shock of the discovery was. Though we all cried and begged her to read no more, she persisted and read us extracts from the Lives of the Lord Chancellors. When she had finished, Jane, the eldest and wisest of us, rose to her feet and said that she for one was not convinced.

"Why," she asked, "if men write such rubbish as this, should our mothers have wasted their youth in bringing them into the world?"

We were all silent; and, in the silence, poor Poll could be heard sobbing out, "Why, why did my father teach me to read?"

Clorinda was the first to come to her senses. "It's all our fault," she said. "Every one of us knows how to read. But no one, save Poll, has ever taken the trouble to do it.

I, for one, have taken it for granted that it was a woman's duty to spend her youth in bearing children. I venerated my mother for bearing ten; still more my grandmother for bearing fifteen; it was, I confess, my own ambition to bear twenty.

We have gone on all these ages supposing that men were equally industrious, and that their works were of equal merit. While we have borne the children, they, we supposed, have borne the books and the pictures.

We have populated the world. They have civilized it. But now that we can read, what prevents us from judging the results? Before we bring another child into the world we must swear that we will find out what the world is like."

So we made ourselves into a society for asking questions. One of us was to visit a man-of-war; another was to hide herself in a scholar's study; another was to attend a meeting of business men; while all were to read books, look at pictures, go to concerts, keep our eyes open in the streets, and ask questions perpetually.

We were very young. You can judge of our simplicity when I tell you that before parting that night we agreed that the objects of life were to produce good people and good books.

Our questions were to be directed to finding out how far these objects were now attained by men. We vowed solemnly that we would not bear a single child until we were satisfied.

Off we went then, some to the British Museum; others to the King's Navy; some to Oxford; others to Cambridge; we visited the Royal Academy and the Tate; heard modern music in concert rooms, went to the Law Courts, and saw new plays.

No one dined out without asking her partner certain questions and carefully noting his replies. At intervals we met together and compared our observations.

Oh, those were merry meeting! Never have I laughed so much as I did when Rose read her notes upon "Honour" and described how she had dressed herself as an Ethiopian Prince and gone aboard one of His Majesty's ships.

Discovering the hoax, the Captain visited her (now disguised as a private gentleman) and demanded that honour should be satisfied.

"But how?" she asked. "How?" he bellowed. "With the cane of course!" Seeing that he was beside himself with rage and expecting that her last moment had come, she bent over and received, to her amazement, six light taps upon the behind.

"The honour of the British Navy is avenged!" he cried, and, raising herself, she saw him with the sweat pouring down his face holding out a trembling right hand.

"Away!" she exclaimed, striking an attitude and imitating the ferocity of his own expression, "My honour has still to be satisfied!" "Spoken like a gentleman!" he returned, and fell into profound thought. "If six strokes avenge the honour of the King's Navy," he mused, "how many avenge the honour of a private gentleman?"

He said he would prefer to lay the case before his brother officers. She replied haughtily that she could not wait. He praised her sensibility.

"Let me see," he cried suddenly, "did your father keep a carriage?" "No," she said. "Or a riding horse?" "We had a donkey," she bethought her, "which drew the mowing machine."

At this his face lighted. "My mother's name——" she added. "For God's sake, man, don't mention your mother's name!" he shrieked, trembling like an aspen and flushing to the roots of his hair, and it was ten minutes at least before she could induce him to proceed.

At length he decreed that if she gave him four strokes and a half in the small of the back at a spot indicated by himself (the half conceded, he said, in recognition of the fact that her great grandmother's uncle was killed at Trafalgar) it was his opinion that her honour would be as good as new.

This was done; they retired to a restaurant; drank two bottles of wine for which he insisted upon paying; and parted with protestations of eternal friendship.

Then we had Fanny's account of her visit to the Law Courts. At her first visit she had come to the conclusion that the Judges were either made of wood or were impersonated by large animals resembling man who had been trained to move with extreme dignity, mumble and nod their heads.

To test her theory she had liberated a handkerchief of bluebottles at the critical moment of a trial, but was unable to judge whether the creatures gave signs of humanity for the buzzing of the flies induced so sound a sleep that she only woke in time to see the prisoners led into the cells below. But from the evidence she brought we voted that it is unfair to suppose that the Judges are men.

Helen went to the Royal Academy, but when asked to deliver her report upon the pictures she began to recite from a pale blue volume, "O! for the touch of a vanished hand and the sound of a voice that is still. Home is the hunter, home from the hill. He gave his bridle reins a shake. Love is sweet, love is brief. Spring, the fair spring, is the year's pleasant King. O! to be in England now that April's there. Men must work and women must weep. The path of duty is the way to glory—" We could listen to no more of this gibberish.

"We want no more poetry!" we cried.

"Daughters of England!" she began, but here we pulled her down, a vase of water getting spilt over her in the scuffle.

"Thank God!" she exclaimed, shaking herself like a dog. "Now I'll roll on the carpet and see if I can't brush off what remains of the Union Jack. Then perhaps—" here she rolled energetically. Getting up she began to explain to us what modern pictures are like when Castalia stopped her.

"What is the average size of a picture?" she asked. "Perhaps two feet by two and a half," she said. Castalia made notes while Helen spoke, and when she had done, and we were trying not to meet each other's eyes, rose and said, "At your wish I spent last week at Oxbridge, disguised as a charwoman. I thus had access to the rooms of several Professors and will now attempt to give you some idea—only," she broke off, "I can't think how to do it. It's all so queer.

These Professors," she went on, "live in large houses built round grass plots each in a kind of cell by himself.

Yet they have every convenience and comfort. You have only to press a button or light a little lamp.

Theirs papers are beautifully filed. Books abound. There are no children or animals, save half a dozen stray cats and one aged bullfinch—a cock. I remember," she broke off, "an Aunt of mine who lived at Dulwich and kept cactuses. You reached the conservatory through the double drawing-room, and there, on the hot pipes, were dozens of them, ugly, squat, bristly little plants each in a separate pot. Once in a hundred years the Aloe flowered, so my Aunt said. But she died before that happened—" We told her to keep to the point.

"Well," she resumed, "when Professor Hobkin was out, I examined his life work, an edition of Sappho. It's a queer looking book, six or seven inches thick, not all by Sappho. Oh, no. Most of it is a defense of Sappho's chastity, which some German had denied, add I can assure you the passion with which these two gentlemen argued, the learning they displayed, the prodigious ingenuity with which they disputed the use of some implement which looked to me for all the world like a hairpin astounded me; especially when the door opened and Professor Hobkin himself appeared. A very nice, mild, old gentleman, but what could he know about chastity?" We misunderstood her.

"No, no," she protested, "he's the soul of honour I'm sure—not that he resembled Rose's sea captain in the least. I was thinking rather of my Aunt's cactuses. What could they know about chastity?"

Again we told her not to wander from the point,— did the Oxbridge professors help to produce good people and good books?—the objects of life.

"There!" she exclaimed. "It never struck me to ask. It never occurred to me that they could possibly produce anything."

"I believe," said Sue, "that you made some mistake. Probably Professor Hobkin was a gynecologist. A scholar is a very different sort of man. A scholar is overflowing with humor and invention—perhaps addicted to wine, but what of that?—a delightful companion, generous, subtle, imaginative—as stands to reason. For he spends his life in company with the finest human beings that have ever existed."

"Hum," said Castalia. "Perhaps I'd better go back and try again."

Some three months later it happened that I was sitting alone when Castalia entered. I don't know what it was in the look of her that so moved me; but I could not restrain myself, and, dashing across the room, I clasped her in my arms. Not only was she very beautiful; she seemed also in the highest spirits. "How happy you look!" I exclaimed, as she sat down.

"I've been at Oxbridge," she said.

"Asking questions?"

"Answering them," she replied.

"You have not broken our vows?" I said anxiously, noticing something about her figure.

"Oh, the vow," she said casually. "I'm going to have a baby, if that's what you mean. You can't imagine," she burst out, "how exciting, how beautiful, how satisfying—"

"What is?" I asked.

"To—to—answer questions," she replied in some confusion. Whereupon she told me the whole of her story. But in the middle of an account which interested and excited me more than anything I had ever heard, she gave the strangest cry, half whoop, half holloa—

"Chastity! Chastity! Where's my chastity!" she cried. "Help Ho! The scent bottle!"

50

There was nothing in the room but a cruet containing mustard, which I was about to administer when she recovered her composure.

"You should have thought of that three months ago," I said severely.

"True," she replied. "There's not much good in thinking of it now. It was unfortunate, by the way, that my mother had me called Castalia."

"Oh, Castalia, your mother—" I was beginning when she reached for the mustard pot.

"No, no, no," she said, shaking her head. "If you'd been a chaste woman yourself you would have screamed at the sight of me—instead of which you rushed across the room and took me in your arms. No, Cassandra. We are neither of us chaste." So we went on talking.

Meanwhile the room was filling up, for it was the day appointed to discuss the results of our observations.

Everyone, I thought, felt as I did about Castalia. They kissed her and said how glad they were to see her again. At length, when we were all assembled, Jane rose and said that it was time to begin.

She began by saying that we had now asked questions for over five years, and that though the results were bound to be inconclusive—here Castalia nudged me and whispered that she was not so sure about that. Then she got up, and, interrupting Jane in the middle of a sentence, said:

"Before you say any more, I want to know—am I to stay in the room? Because," she added, "I have to confess that I am an impure woman."

Everyone looked at her in astonishment.

"You are going to have a baby?" asked Jane.

She nodded her head.

It was extraordinary to see the different expressions on their faces. A sort of hum went through the room, in which I could catch the words "impure," "baby," "Castalia," and so on. Jane, who was herself considerably moved, put it to us:

"Shall she go? Is she impure?"

Such a roar filled the room as might have been heard in the street outside.

"No! No! No! Let her stay! Impure? Fiddlesticks!" Yet I fancied that some of the youngest, girls of nineteen or twenty, held back as if overcome with shyness.

Then we all came about her and began asking questions, and at last I saw one of the youngest, who had kept in the background, approach shyly and say to her:

"What is chastity then? I mean is it good, or is it bad, or is it nothing at all?" She replied so low that I could not catch what she said.

"You know I was shocked," said another, "for at least ten minutes."

"In my opinion," said Poll, who was growing crusty from always reading in the London Library, "chastity is nothing but ignorance—a most discreditable state of mind. We should admit only the unchaste to our society. I vote that Castalia shall be our President."

This was violently disputed.

"It is as unfair to brand women with chastity as with unchastity," said Poll. "Some of us haven't the opportunity either. Moreover, I don't believe Cassy herself maintains that she acted as she did from a pure love of knowledge."

"He is only twenty-one and divinely beautiful," said Cassy, with a ravishing gesture.

"I move," said Helen, "that no one be allowed to talk of chastity or unchastity save those who are in love."

"Oh, bother," said Judith, who had been inquiring into scientific matters, "I'm not in love and I'm longing to explain my measures for dispensing with prostitutes and fertilizing virgins by Act of Parliament."

She went on to tell us of an invention of hers to be erected at Tube stations and other public resorts, which, upon payment of a small fee, would safeguard the nation's health, accommodate its sons, and relieve its daughters.

Then she had contrived a method of preserving in sealed tubes the germs of future Lord Chancellors "or poets or painters or musicians," she went on, "supposing, that is to say, that these breeds are not extinct, and that women still wish to bear children ____"

"Of course we wish to bear children!" cried Castalia, impatiently. Jane rapped the table.

"That is the very point we are met to consider," she said. "For five years we have been trying to find out whether we are justified in continuing the human race. Castalia has anticipated our decision. But it remains for the rest of us to make up our minds."

Here one after another of our messengers rose and delivered their reports. The marvels of civilization far exceeded our expectations, and, as we learnt for the first time how man flies in the air, talks across space, penetrates to the heart of an atom, and embraces the universe in his speculations, a murmur of admiration burst from our lips.

"We are proud," we cried, "that our mothers sacrificed their youth in such a cause as this!" Castalia, who had been listening intently, looked prouder than all the rest.

Then Jane reminded us that we had still much to learn, and Castalia begged us to make haste. On we went through a vast tangle of statistics.

We learnt that England has a population of so many millions, and that such and such a proportion of them is constantly hungry and in prison; that the average size of a working man's family is such, and that so great a percentage of women die from maladies incident to childbirth.

Reports were read of visits to factories, shops, slums, and dockyards. Descriptions were given of the Stock Exchange, of a gigantic house of business in the City, and of a Government Office.

The British Colonies were now discussed, and some account was given of our rule in India, Africa and Ireland. I was sitting by Castalia and I noticed her uneasiness.

"We shall never come to any conclusion at all at this rate," she said. "As it appears that civilization is so much more complex than we had any notion, would it not be better to confine ourselves to our original inquiry?

We agreed that it was the object of life to produce good people and good books. All this time we have been talking of aeroplanes, factories, and money. Let us talk about men themselves and their arts, for that is the heart of the matter."

So the diners out stepped forward with long slips of paper containing answers to their questions. These had been framed after much consideration.

A good man, we had agreed, must at any rate be honest, passionate, and unworldly. But whether or not a particular man possessed those qualities could only be discovered by asking questions, often beginning at a remote distance from the center.

Is Kensington a nice place to live in? Where is your son being educated—and your daughter? Now please tell me, what do you pay for your cigars? By the way, is Sir Joseph a baronet or only a knight?

Often it seemed that we learnt more from trivial questions of this kind than from more direct ones.

"I accepted my peerage," said Lord Bunkum, "because my wife wished it." I forget how many titles were accepted for the same reason.

"Working fifteen hours out of the twenty-four, as I do——" ten thousand professional men began.

"No, no, of course you can neither read nor write. But why do you work so hard?" "My dear lady, with a growing family——"

"But why does your family grow?" Their wives wished that too, or perhaps it was the British Empire.

But more significant than the answers were the refusals to answer. Very few would reply at all to questions about morality and religion, and such answers as were given were not serious.

Questions as to the value of money and power were almost invariably brushed aside, or pressed at extreme risk to the asker.

"I'm sure," said Jill, "that if Sir Harley Tightboots hadn't been carving the mutton when I asked him about the capitalist system he would have cut my throat.

The only reason why we escaped with our lives over and over again is that men are at once so hungry and so chivalrous. They despise us too much to mind what we say."

"Of course they despise us," said Eleanor. "At the same time how do you account for this—I made inquiries among the artists. Now, no woman has ever been an artist, has she, Polls?"

"Jane Austen - Charlotte Brontë - George Eliot," cried Poll, like a man crying muffins in a back street. "Damn the woman!" someone exclaimed. "What a bore she is!"

"Since Sappho there has been no female of first rate
——" Eleanor began, quoting from a weekly
newspaper.

"It's now well known that Sappho was the
somewhat lewd invention of Professor Hobkin," Ruth
interrupted.

"Anyhow, there is no reason to suppose that any
woman ever has been able to write or ever will be able
to write," Eleanor continued. "And yet, whenever I go
among authors they never cease to talk to me about
their books. Masterly! I say, or Shakespeare himself!
(for one must say something) and I assure you, they
believe me."

"That proves nothing," said Jane. "They all do it.
Only," she sighed, "it doesn't seem to help us much.
Perhaps we had better examine modern literature
next. Liz, it's your turn."

Elizabeth rose and said that in order to prosecute
her inquiry she had dressed as a man and been taken
for a reviewer.

"I have read new books pretty steadily for the past
five years," said she. "Mr. Wells is the most popular
living writer; then comes Mr. Arnold Bennett; then Mr.
Compton Makenzie; Mr. McKenna and Mr. Walpole
may be bracketed together." She sat down.

"But you've told us nothing!" we expostulated. "Or
do you mean that these gentlemen have greatly
surpassed Jane-Elliot and that English fiction is——
where's that review of yours? Oh, yes, 'safe in their
hands.'"

"Safe, quite safe," she said, shifting uneasily from
foot to foot. "And I'm sure that they give away even
more than they receive."

We were all sure of that. "But," we pressed her, "do
they write good books?"

"Good books?" she said, looking at the ceiling "You

must remember," she began, speaking with extreme rapidity, "that fiction is the mirror of life. And you can't deny that education is of the highest importance, and that it would be extremely annoying, if you found yourself alone at Brighton late at night, not to know which was the best boarding house to stay at, and suppose it was a dripping Sunday evening—wouldn't it be nice to go to the Movies?"

"But what has that got to do with it?" we asked.

"Nothing—nothing—nothing whatever," she replied.

"Well, tell us the truth," we bade her.

"The truth? But isn't it wonderful," she broke off —"Mr. Chitter has written a weekly article for the past thirty years upon love or hot buttered toast and has sent all his sons to Eton——"

"The truth!" we demanded.

"Oh, the truth," she stammered, "the truth has nothing to do with literature," and sitting down she refused to say another word.

It all seemed to us very inconclusive.

"Ladies, we must try to sum up the results," Jane was beginning, when a hum, which had been heard for some time through the open window, drowned her voice.

"War! War! War! Declaration of War!" men were shouting in the street below.

We looked at each other in horror.

"What war?" we cried. "What war?" We remembered, too late, that we had never thought of sending anyone to the House of Commons. We had forgotten all about it.

We turned to Poll, who had reached the history shelves in the London Library, and asked her to enlighten us.

"Why," we cried, "do men go to war?"

"Sometimes for one reason, sometimes for another," she replied calmly. "In 1760, for example——" The shouts outside drowned her words. "Again in 1797—in 1804—It was the Austrians in 1866—1870 was the Franco-Prussian—In 1900 on the other hand——"

"But it's now 1914!" we cut her short.

"Ah, I don't know what they're going to war for now," she admitted.

The war was over and peace was in process of being signed, when I once more found myself with Castalia in the room where our meetings used to be held.

We began idly turning over the pages of our old minute books. "Queer," I mused, "to see what we were thinking five years ago."

"We are agreed," Castalia quoted, reading over my shoulder, "that it is the object of life to produce good people and good books." We made no comment upon that. "A good man is at any rate honest, passionate and unworldly."

"What a woman's language!" I observed.

"Oh, dear," cried Castalia, pushing the book away from her, "what fools we were! It was all Poll's father's fault," she went on. "I believe he did it on purpose—that ridiculous will, I mean, forcing Poll to read all the books in the London Library. If we hadn't learnt to read," she said bitterly, "we might still have been bearing children in ignorance and that I believe was the happiest life after all."

"I know what you're going to say about war," she checked me, "and the horror of bearing children to see them killed, but our mothers did it, and their mothers, and their mothers before them.

And they didn't complain. They couldn't read. I've done my best," she sighed, "to prevent my little girl from learning to read, but what's the use?"

"I caught Ann only yesterday with a newspaper in her hand and she was beginning to ask me if it was 'true.' Next she'll ask me whether Mr. Lloyd George is a good man, then whether Mr. Arnold Bennett is a good novelist, and finally whether I believe in God. How can I bring my daughter up to believe in nothing?" she demanded.

"Surely you could teach her to believe that a man's intellect is, and always will be, fundamentally superior to a woman's?" I suggested.

She brightened at this and began to turn over our old minutes again.

"Yes," she said, "think of their discoveries, their mathematics, their science, their philosophy, their scholarship——" and then she began to laugh, "I shall never forget old Hobkin and the hairpin," she said, and went on reading and laughing and I thought she was quite happy, when suddenly she drew the book from her and burst out, "Oh, Cassandra, why do you torment me? Don't you know that our belief in man's intellect is the greatest fallacy of them all?"

"What?" I exclaimed. "Ask any journalist, schoolmaster, politician or public house keeper in the land and they will all tell you that men are much cleverer than women."

"As if I doubted it," she said scornfully. "How could they help it? Haven't we bred them and fed and kept them in comfort since the beginning of time so that they may be clever even if they're nothing else? It's all our doing!" she cried.

"We insisted upon having intellect and now we've got it. And it's intellect," she continued, "that's at the bottom of it. What could be more charming than a boy before he has begun to cultivate his intellect? He is beautiful to look at; he gives himself no airs; he understands the meaning of art and literature instinctively; he goes about enjoying his life and making other people enjoy theirs.

Then they teach him to cultivate his intellect. He becomes a barrister, a civil servant, a general, an author, a professor.

Every day he goes to an office. Every year he produces a book. He maintains a whole family by the products of his brain—poor devil!

Soon he cannot come into a room without making us all feel uncomfortable; he condescends to every woman he meets, and dares not tell the truth even to his own wife; instead of rejoicing our eyes we have to shut them if we are to take him in our arms.

True, they console themselves with stars of all shapes, ribbons of all shades, and incomes of all sizes —but what is to console us? That we shall be able in ten years' time to spend a weekend at Lahore? Or that the least insect in Japan has a name twice the length of its body?

Oh, Cassandra, for Heaven's sake let us devise a method by which men may bear children! It is our only chance. For unless we provide them with some innocent occupation we shall get neither good people nor good books; we shall perish beneath the fruits of their unbridled activity; and not a human being will survive to know that there once was Shakespeare!"

"It is too late," I replied. "We cannot provide even for the children that we have."

"And then you ask me to believe in intellect," she said.

While we spoke, man were crying hoarsely and wearily in the street, and, listening, we heard that the Treaty of Peace had just been signed.

The voices died away. The rain was falling and interfered no doubt with the proper explosion of the fireworks.

"My cook will have bought the Evening News," said Castalia, "and Ann will be spelling it out over her tea. I must go home."

"It's no good—not a bit of good," I said. "Once she knows how to read there's only one thing you can teach her to believe in—and that is herself."

"Well, that would be a change," sighed Castalia.

So we swept up the papers of our Society, and, though Ann was playing with her doll very happily, we solemnly made her a present of the lot and told her we had chosen her to be President of the Society of the future—upon which she burst into tears, poor little girl.

* * * * *

Kew Gardens

FROM the oval-shaped flower-bed there rose perhaps a hundred stalks spreading into heart-shaped or tongue-shaped leaves half way up and unfurling at the tip red or blue or yellow petals marked with spots of color raised upon the surface; and from the red, blue or yellow gloom of the throat emerged a straight bar, rough with gold dust and slightly clubbed at the end.

The petals were voluminous enough to be stirred by the summer breeze, and when they moved, the red, blue and yellow lights passed one over the other, staining an inch of the brown earth beneath with a spot of the most intricate color.

The light fell either upon the smooth, grey back of a pebble, or, the shell of a snail with its brown, circular veins, or falling into a raindrop, it expanded with such intensity of red, blue and yellow the thin walls of water that one expected them to burst and disappear.

Instead, the drop was left in a second silver grey once more, and the light now settled upon the flesh of a leaf, revealing the branching thread of fiber beneath the surface, and again it moved on and spread its illumination in the vast green spaces beneath the dome of the heart-shaped and tongue-shaped leaves.

Then the breeze stirred rather more briskly overhead and the color was flashed into the air above, into the eyes of the men and women who walk in Kew Gardens in July.

The figures of these men and women straggled past

the flower-bed with a curiously irregular movement not unlike that of the white and blue butterflies who crossed the turf in zig-zag flights from bed to bed.

The man was about six inches in front of the woman, strolling carelessly, while she bore on with greater purpose, only turning her head now and then to see that the children were not too far behind.

The man kept this distance in front of the woman purposely, though perhaps unconsciously, for he wished to go on with his thoughts.

"Fifteen years ago I came here with Lily," he thought. "We sat somewhere over there by a lake and I begged her to marry me all through the hot afternoon.

How the dragonfly kept circling round us: how clearly I see the dragonfly and her shoe with the square silver buckle at the toe.

All the time I spoke I saw her shoe and when it moved impatiently I knew without looking up what she was going to say: the whole of her seemed to be in her shoe.

And my love, my desire, were in the dragonfly; for some reason I thought that if it settled there, on that leaf, the broad one with the red flower in the middle of it, if the dragonfly settled on the leaf she would say "Yes" at once.

But the dragonfly went round and round: it never settled anywhere—of course not, happily not, or I shouldn't be walking here with Eleanor and the children—Tell me, Eleanor. Do you ever think of the past?"

"Why do you ask, Simon?"

"Because I've been thinking of the past. I've been thinking of Lily, the woman I might have married... Well, why are you silent? Do you mind my thinking of the past?"

"Why should I mind, Simon? Doesn't one always

think of the past, in a garden with men and women lying under the trees? Aren't they one's past, all that remains of it, those men and women, those ghosts lying under the trees,... one's happiness, one's reality?"

"For me, a square silver shoe buckle and a dragonfly—"

"For me, a kiss. Imagine six little girls sitting before their easels twenty years ago, down by the side of a lake, painting the water-lilies, the first red water-lilies I'd ever seen. And suddenly a kiss, there on the back of my neck. And my hand shook all the afternoon so that I couldn't paint.

I took out my watch and marked the hour when I would allow myself to think of the kiss for five minutes only—it was so precious—the kiss of an old grey-haired woman with a wart on her nose, the mother of all my kisses all my life. Come, Caroline, come, Hubert."

They walked on the past the flower—bed, now walking four abreast, and soon diminished in size among the trees and looked half transparent as the sunlight and shade swam over their backs in large trembling irregular patches.

In the oval flower bed the snail, whose shell had been stained red, blue, and yellow for the space of two minutes or so, now appeared to be moving very slightly in its shell, and next began to labor over the crumbs of loose earth which broke away and rolled down as it passed over them.

It appeared to have a definite goal in front of it, differing in this respect from the singular high stepping angular green insect who attempted to cross in front of it, and waited for a second with its antenna trembling as if in deliberation, and then stepped off as rapidly and strangely in the opposite direction.

Brown cliffs with deep green lakes in the hollows, flat, blade-like trees that waved from root to tip, round boulders of grey stone, vast crumpled surfaces of a thin crackling texture—all these objects lay across the snail's progress between one stalk and another to his goal.

Before he had decided whether to circumvent the arched tent of a dead leaf or to breast it there came past the bed the feet of other human beings.

This time they were both men. The younger of the two wore an expression of perhaps unnatural calm; he raised his eyes and fixed them very steadily in front of him while his companion spoke, and directly his companion had done speaking he looked on the ground again and sometimes opened his lips only after a long pause and sometimes did not open them at all.

The elder man had a curiously uneven and shaky method of walking, jerking his hand forward and throwing up his head abruptly, rather in the manner of an impatient carriage horse tired of waiting outside a house; but in the man these gestures were irresolute and pointless.

He talked almost incessantly; he smiled to himself and again began to talk, as if the smile had been an answer. He was talking about spirits—the spirits of the dead, who, according to him, were even now telling him all sorts of odd things about their experiences in Heaven.

"Heaven was known to the ancients as Thessaly, William, and now, with this war, the spirit matter is rolling between the hills like thunder." He paused, seemed to listen, smiled, jerked his head and continued:—

"You have a small electric battery and a piece of rubber to insulate the wire—isolate?—insulate?—well, we'll skip the details, no good going into details that wouldn't be understood—and in short the little machine stands in any convenient position by the head of the bed, we will say, on a neat mahogany stand.

All arrangements being properly fixed by workmen under my direction, the widow applies her ear and summons the spirit by sign as agreed. Women! Widows! Women in black——"

Here he seemed to have caught sight of a woman's dress in the distance, which in the shade looked a purple black. He took off his hat, placed his hand upon his heart, and hurried towards her muttering and gesticulating feverishly.

But William caught him by the sleeve and touched a flower with the tip of his walking-stick in order to divert the old man's attention.

After looking at it for a moment in some confusion the old man bent his ear to it and seemed to answer a voice speaking from it, for he began talking about the forests of Uruguay which he had visited hundreds of years ago in company with the most beautiful young woman in Europe.

He could be heard murmuring about forests of Uruguay blanketed with the wax petals of tropical roses, nightingales, sea beaches, mermaids, and women drowned at sea, as he suffered himself to be moved on by William, upon whose face the look of stoical patience grew slowly deeper and deeper.

Following his steps so closely as to be slightly puzzled by his gestures came two elderly women of the lower middle class, one stout and ponderous, the other rosy cheeked and nimble.

Like most people of their station they were frankly fascinated by any signs of eccentricity betokening a disordered brain, especially in the well-to-do; but they were too far off to be certain whether the gestures were merely eccentric or genuinely mad. After they had scrutinized the old man's back in silence for a moment and given each other a queer, sly look, they went on energetically piecing together their very complicated dialogue:

"Nell, Bert, Lot, Cess, Phil, Pa, he says, I says, she says, I says, I says, I says——"

"My Bert, Sis, Bill, Grandad, the old man, sugar,

Sugar, flour, kippers, greens,

Sugar, sugar, sugar."

The ponderous woman looked through the pattern of falling words at the flowers standing cool, firm, and upright in the earth, with a curious expression. She saw them as a sleeper waking from a heavy sleep sees a brass candlestick reflecting the light in an unfamiliar way, and closes his eyes and opens them, and seeing the brass candlestick again, finally starts broad awake and stares at the candlestick with all his powers.

So the heavy woman came to a standstill opposite the oval-shaped flower bed, and ceased even to pretend to listen to what the other woman was saying. She stood there letting the words fall over her, swaying the top part of her body slowly backwards and forwards, looking at the flowers. Then she suggested that they should find a seat and have their tea.

The snail had now considered every possible method of reaching his goal without going round the dead leaf or climbing over it. Let alone the effort needed for climbing a leaf, he was doubtful whether the thin texture which vibrated with such an alarming crackle when touched even by the tip of his horns would bear his weight; and this determined him finally to creep beneath it, for there was a point where the leaf curved high enough from the ground to admit him.

He had just inserted his head in the opening and was taking stock of the high brown roof and was getting used to the cool brown light when two other people came past outside on the turf.

This time they were both young, a young man and a young woman. They were both in the prime of youth, or even in that season which precedes the prime of youth, the season before the smooth pink folds of the flower have burst their gummy case, when the wings of the butterfly, though fully grown, are motionless in the sun.

"Lucky it isn't Friday," he observed.

"Why? Do you believe in luck?"

"They make you pay sixpence on Friday."

"What's sixpence anyway? Isn't it worth sixpence?"

"What's 'it'—what do you mean by 'it'?"

"O, anything—I mean—you know what I mean."

Long pauses came between each of these remarks; they were uttered in toneless and monotonous voices.

The couple stood still on the edge of the flower bed, and together pressed the end of her parasol deep down into the soft earth.

The action and the fact that his hand rested on the top of hers expressed their feelings in a strange way, as these short insignificant words also expressed something, words with short wings for their heavy body of meaning, inadequate to carry them far and thus alighting awkwardly upon the very common objects that surrounded them, and were to their inexperienced touch so massive; but who knows (so they thought as they pressed the parasol into the earth) what precipices aren't concealed in them, or what slopes of ice don't shine in the sun on the other side? Who knows? Who has ever seen this before?

Even when she wondered what sort of tea they gave you at Kew, he felt that something loomed up behind her words, and stood vast and solid behind them; and the mist very slowly rose and uncovered—O, Heavens, what were those shapes?—little white tables, and waitresses who looked first at her and then at him; and there was a bill that he would pay with a real two shilling piece, and it was real, all real, he assured himself, fingering the coin in his pocket, real to everyone except to him and to her; even to him it began to seem real; and then—but it was too exciting to stand and think any longer, and he pulled the parasol out of the earth with a jerk and was impatient to find the place where one had tea with other people, like other people.

"Come along, Trissie; it's time we had our tea."

"Wherever does one have one's tea?" she asked with the oddest thrill of excitement in her voice, looking vaguely round and letting herself be drawn on down the grass path, trailing her parasol, turning her head this way and that way, forgetting her tea, wishing to go down there and then down there, remembering orchids and cranes among wild flowers, a Chinese pagoda and a crimson crested bird; but he bore her on.

Thus one couple after another with much the same irregular and aimless movement passed the flower-bed and were enveloped in layer after layer of green blue vapor, in which at first their bodies had substance and a dash of color, but later both substance and color dissolved in the green-blue atmosphere.

How hot it was! So hot that even the thrush chose to hop, like a mechanical bird, in the shadow of the flowers, with long pauses between one movement and the next; instead of rambling vaguely the white butterflies danced one above another, making with their white shifting flakes the outline of a shattered marble column above the tallest flowers the glass roofs of the palm house shone as if a whole market full of shiny green umbrellas had opened in the sun; and in the drone of the aeroplane the voice of the summer sky murmured its fierce soul. Yellow and black, pink and snow white, shapes of all these colors, men, women, and children were spotted for a second upon the horizon, and then, seeing the breadth of yellow that lay upon the grass, they wavered and sought shade beneath the trees, dissolving like drops of water in the yellow and green atmosphere, staining it faintly with red and blue.

It seemed as if all gross and heavy bodies had sunk down in the heat motionless and lay huddled upon the ground, but their voices went wavering from them as if they were flames lolling from the thick waxen bodies of candles.

Voices. Yes, voices. Wordless voices, breaking the silence suddenly with such depth of contentment, such passion of desire, or, in the voices of children, such freshness of surprise; breaking the silence?

But there was no silence; all the time the motor omnibuses were turning their wheels and changing their gear; like a vast nest of Chinese boxes all of wrought steel turning ceaselessly one within another the city murmured; on the top of which the voices cried aloud and the petals of myriads of flowers flashed their colors into the air.

* * * * *

Solid Objects

The only thing that moved upon the vast semicircle of the beach was one small black spot. As it came nearer to the ribs and spine of the stranded pilchard boat, it became apparent from a certain tenuity in its blackness that this spot possessed four legs; and moment by moment it became more unmistakable that it was composed of the persons of two young men.

Even thus in outline against the sand there was an unmistakable vitality in them; an indescribable vigor in the approach and withdrawal of the bodies, slight though it was, which proclaimed some violent argument issuing from the tiny mouths of the little round heads.

This was corroborated on closer view by the repeated lunging of a walking-stick on the right-hand side. "You mean to tell me . . . You actually believe . . . " thus the walking-stick on the right-hand side next the waves seemed to be asserting as it cut long straight stripes upon the sand.

"Politics be damned!" issued clearly from the body on the left-hand side, and, as these words were uttered, the mouths, noses, chins, little mustaches, tweed caps, rough boots, shooting coats, and check stockings of the two speakers became clearer and clearer; the smoke of their pipes went up into the air; nothing was so solid, so living, so hard, red, hirsute and virile as these two bodies for miles and miles of sea and sand hill.

They flung themselves down by the six ribs and spine of the black pilchard boat. You know how the body seems to shake itself free from an argument, and to apologize for a mood of exaltation; flinging itself down and expressing in the looseness of its attitude a readiness to take up with something new—whatever it may be that comes next to hand.

So Charles, whose stick had been slashing the beach for half a mile or so, began skimming flat pieces of slate over the water; and John, who had exclaimed "Politics be damned!" began burrowing his fingers down, down, into the sand.

As his hand went further and further beyond the wrist, so that he had to hitch his sleeve a little higher, his eyes lost their intensity, or rather the background of thought and experience which gives an inscrutable depth to the eyes of grown people disappeared, leaving only the clear transparent surface, expressing nothing but wonder, which the eyes of young children display.

No doubt the act of burrowing in the sand had something to do with it. He remembered that, after digging for a little, the water oozes round your finger-tips; the hole then becomes a moat; a well; a spring; a secret channel to the sea.

As he was choosing which of these things to make it, still working his fingers in the water, they curled round something hard—a full drop of solid matter—and gradually dislodged a large irregular lump, and brought it to the surface.

When the sand coating was wiped off, a green tint appeared. It was a lump of glass, so thick as to be almost opaque; the smoothing of the sea had completely worn off any edge or shape, so that it was impossible to say whether it had been bottle, tumbler or window-pane; it was nothing but glass; it was almost a precious stone.

You had only to enclose it in a rim of gold, or pierce it with a wire, and it became a jewel; part of a necklace, or a dull, green light upon a finger.

Perhaps after all it was really a gem; something worn by a dark Princess trailing her finger in the water as she sat in the stern of the boat and listened to the slaves singing as they rowed her across the Bay.

Or the oak sides of a sunk Elizabethan treasure-chest had split apart, and, rolled over and over, over and over, its emeralds had come at last to shore.

John turned it in his hands; he held it to the light; he held it so that its irregular mass blotted out the body and extended right arm of his friend. The green thinned and thickened slightly as it was held against the sky or against the body.

It pleased him; it puzzled him; it was so hard, so concentrated, so definite an object compared with the vague sea and the hazy shore.

Now a sigh disturbed him—profound, final, making him aware that his friend Charles had thrown all the flat stones within reach, or had come to the conclusion that it was not worth while to throw them.

They ate their sandwiches side by side. When they had done, and were shaking themselves and rising to their feet, John took the lump of glass and looked at it in silence.

Charles looked at it too. But he saw immediately that it was not flat, and filling his pipe he said with the energy that dismisses a foolish strain of thought:

"To return to what I was saying——"

He did not see, or if he had seen would hardly have noticed, that John, after looking at the lump for a moment, as if in hesitation, slipped it inside his pocket.

That impulse, too, may have been the impulse

which leads a child to pick up one pebble on a path strewn with them, promising it a life of warmth and security upon the nursery mantelpiece, delighting in the sense of power and benignity which such an action confers, and believing that the heart of the stone leaps with joy when it sees itself chosen from a million like it, to enjoy this bliss instead of a life of cold and wet upon the high road.

"It might so easily have been any other of the millions of stones, but it was I, I, I!"

Whether this thought or not was in John's mind, the lump of glass had its place upon the mantelpiece, where it stood heavy upon a little pile of bills and letters and served not only as an excellent paper-weight, but also as a natural stopping place for the young man's eyes when they wandered from his book.

Looked at again and again half consciously by a mind thinking of something else, any object mixes itself so profoundly with the stuff of thought that it loses its actual form and recomposes itself a little differently in an ideal shape which haunts the brain when we least expect it.

So John found himself attracted to the windows of curiosity shops when he was out walking, merely because he saw something which reminded him of the lump of glass.

Anything, so long as it was an object of some kind, more or less round, perhaps with a dying flame deep sunk in its mass, anything—china, glass, amber, rock, marble—even the smooth oval egg of a prehistoric bird would do.

He took, also, to keeping his eyes upon the ground, especially in the neighborhood of waste land where the household refuse is thrown away. Such objects often occurred there—thrown away, of no use to anybody, shapeless, discarded.

In a few months he had collected four or five specimens that took their place upon the mantelpiece. They were useful, too, for a man who is standing for Parliament upon the brink of a brilliant career has any number of papers to keep in order—addresses to constituents, declarations of policy, appeals for subscriptions, invitations to dinner, and so on.

One day, starting from his rooms in the Temple to catch a train in order to address his constituents, his eyes rested upon a remarkable object lying half-hidden in one of those little borders of grass which edge the bases of vast legal buildings.

He could only touch it with the point of his stick through the railings; but he could see that it was a piece of china of the most remarkable shape, as nearly resembling a starfish as anything—shaped, or broken accidentally, into five irregular but unmistakable points.

The coloring was mainly blue, but green stripes or spots of some kind overlaid the blue, and lines of crimson gave it a richness and luster of the most attractive kind.

John was determined to possess it; but the more he pushed, the further it receded. At length he was forced to go back to his rooms and improvise a wire ring attached to the end of a stick, with which, by dint of great care and skill, he finally drew the piece of china within reach of his hands.

As he seized hold of it he exclaimed in triumph. At that moment the clock struck. It was out of the question that he should keep his appointment. The meeting was held without him.

But how had the piece of china been broken into this remarkable shape?

A careful examination put it beyond doubt that the star shape was accidental, which made it all the more strange, and it seemed unlikely that there should be another such in existence.

Set at the opposite end of the mantelpiece from the lump of glass that had been dug from the sand, it looked like a creature from another world—freakish and fantastic as a harlequin.

It seemed to be pirouetting through space, winking light like a fitful star. The contrast between the china so vivid and alert, and the glass so mute and contemplative, fascinated him, and wondering and amazed he asked himself how the two came to exist in the same world, let alone to stand upon the same narrow strip of marble in the same room. The question remained unanswered.

He now began to haunt the places which are most prolific of broken china, such as pieces of waste land between railway lines, sites of demolished houses, and commons in the neighborhood of London.

But china is seldom thrown from a great height; it is one of the rarest of human actions. You have to find in conjunction a very high house, and a woman of such reckless impulse and passionate prejudice that she flings her jar or pot straight from the window without thought of who is below.

Broken china was to be found in plenty, but broken in some trifling domestic accident, without purpose or character. Nevertheless, he was often astonished as he came to go into the question more deeply, by the immense variety of shapes to be found in London alone, and there was still more cause for wonder and speculation in the differences of qualities and designs.

The finest specimens he would bring home and place upon his mantelpiece, where, however, their duty was more and more of an ornamental nature, since papers needing a weight to keep them down became scarcer and scarcer.

He neglected his duties, perhaps, or discharged them absentmindedly, or his constituents when they visited him were unfavorably impressed by the appearance of his mantelpiece.

At any rate he was not elected to represent them in Parliament, and his friend Charles, taking it much to heart and hurrying to condole with him, found him so little cast down by the disaster that he could only suppose that it was too serious a matter for him to realize all at once.

In truth, John had been that day to Barnes Common, and there under a furze bush had found a very remarkable piece of iron.

It was almost identical with the glass in shape, massy and globular, but so cold and heavy, so black and metallic, that it was evidently alien to the earth and had its origin in one of the dead stars or was itself the cinder of a moon.

It weighed his pocket down; it weighed the mantelpiece down; it radiated cold. And yet the meteorite stood upon the same ledge with the lump of glass and the star-shaped china.

As his eyes passed from one to another, the determination to possess objects that even surpassed these tormented the young man. He devoted himself more and more resolutely to the search.

If he had not been consumed by ambition and convinced that one day some newly-discovered rubbish heap would reward him, the disappointments he had suffered, let alone the fatigue and derision, would have made him give up the pursuit.

Provided with a bag and a long stick fitted with an adaptable hook, he ransacked all deposits of earth; raked beneath matted tangles of scrub; searched all alleys and spaces between walls where he had learned to expect to find objects of this kind thrown away.

As his standard became higher and his taste more severe the disappointments were innumerable, but always some gleam of hope, some piece of china or glass curiously marked or broken lured him on.

Day after day passed. He was no longer young. His career—that is his political career—was a thing of the past. People gave up visiting him. He was too silent to be worth asking to dinner. He never talked to anyone about his serious ambitions; their lack of understanding was apparent in their behavior.

He leaned back in his chair now and watched Charles lift the stones on the mantelpiece a dozen times and put them down emphatically to mark what he was saying about the conduct of the Government, without once noticing their existence.

"What was the truth of it, John?" asked Charles suddenly, turning and facing him. "What made you give it up like that all in a second?"

"I've not given it up," John replied.

"But you've not the ghost of a chance now," said Charles roughly.

"I don't agree with you there," said John with conviction. Charles looked at him and was profoundly uneasy; the most extraordinary doubts possessed him; he had a queer sense that they were talking about different things.

He looked round to find some relief for his horrible depression, but the disorderly appearance of the room depressed him still further.

What was that stick, and the old carpet bag hanging against the wall? And then those stones?

Looking at John, something fixed and distant in his expression alarmed him. He knew only too well that his mere appearance upon a platform was out of the question.

"Pretty stones," he said as cheerfully as he could; and saying that he had an appointment to keep, he left John—for ever.

* * * * *

Virginia Woolf

Annotations

The String Quartet

Landaus with bays

Four-wheeled enclosed carriages pulled by dark reddish-brown horses.

Regent Street

Regent Street is one of the principal shopping streets in London. The central, curved portion of the street between Piccadilly Circus and Oxford Street is known as the Quadrant.

The Treaty signed

The Treaty of Versailles signed on June 28th, 1918 between Germany and the allies and brought a formal end to World War I.

Influenza

Refers to the influenza pandemic of 1918-1919 that killed over 230,000 Britons and well over 20 million people worldwide.

The King

George V, the King of the United Kingdom (reigned 1910-1938)

Malmesbury

A small town in Wiltshire, a county in South West England.

An Unwritten Novel

The map of the line framed opposite

The story takes place on a train journey from London to Sussex, and there is a framed map of line above the narrator's seat. Three Bridges and Lewes, mentioned a little further in the story, are stops on a line which Woolf knew well from traveling between her homes in London and Sussex.

Croydon

A small town in West Sussex.

Travels in-- shall we say buttons?

He is probably a traveling salesman of buttons.

He reads "Truth"

A weekly newspaper published between 1877 and 1957.

The Mark on the Wall

Chrysanthemums

Chrysanthemums, sometimes called mums or chrysanths, are flowering plants of the genus Chrysanthemum in the family Asteraceae. They are native to Asia and northeastern Europe. Most species originate from East Asia and the center of diversity is in China. There are countless horticultural varieties and cultivars.

Cavalcade

A cavalcade is a formal procession or parade of people walking, on horseback, or riding in vehicles; eg "the royal cavalcade proceeded through the city".

Asphodel meadows

Asphodel is a flowering plant of the lily family associated with death in Greek mythology. Asphodel meadows is a section of the Ancient Greek underworld where ordinary souls were sent to live after death in Homer's Odyssey.

Troy three times over

Troy was ancient fortress city situated near the Dardanelles Asia Minor. Troy was captured and sacked by the Greeks who tricked the Trojans with their wooden horse trick around 1184 BC. By the time Woolf wrote this story, excavations at Troy had revealed no fewer than nine superimposed cities.

Kingsway

Kingsway is a thoroughfare in central London open in 1905 by Edward VII (reigned 1901-1910) and named in his honour. It was conceived in response to Victorian traffic congestion. It turns north-south between the Aldwych and Holborn.

Charles the First

Charles I reigned from 1625 to 1649, when he was beheaded.

Whitaker's Table of Precedency

In every edition of Whitaker's Almanack, a reference book, published annually in the United Kingdom since 1868, there is a "Table of Precedency" which sets out a social hierarchy from the "Sovereign" down to "Naval, Military, Air, and Other Esquires by Office".

Landseer prints

Sir Edwin Landseer (1802-1873) became celebrated for his sentimental paintings of animals. Many of his most popular images enjoyed mass circulation in the form of prints.

The South Downs

The treeless chalk uplands forming a ridge across the southern English counties of Sussex and Hampshire.

Blue & Green

Lustre

Decorative prismatic glass pendants attached to a chandelier or other ornament.

A Society

London Library

Virginia Woolf's father, Sir Leslie Stephen, was the fifth President of the Library which was founded in 1841.

"From a Window"

The title and names suggest that it is "From a College Window" by the novelist A. C. Benson.

Dulwich

Dulwich village is an affluent district in south-east London

Cassandra

In Greek myth, Cassandra was the prophetic daughter of King Priam of Troy. It was Cassandra's fate to always prophesy truthfully but never to be believed.

Kew Gardens

Kew Gardens

Kew Gardens is a botanical garden in southwest London that houses the largest and most diverse botanical and mycological collections in the world.

Thessaly

Historically, a fertile area in north-eastern Greece known for its magicians.

* * * * *

String Quartet

www.ingramcontent.com/pod-product-compliance
Lightning Source LLC
Chambersburg PA
CBHW070349130626
46556CB00007B/3088

* 9 7 8 1 9 4 3 3 4 1 0 2 3 *